JIM NASIUM

STONE ARCH BOOKS

a capstone imprint

Jim Nasium
is published by Stone Arch Books,
a Capstone Imprint
1710 Roe Crest Drive
North Mankato, Minnesota 56003
www.capstoneyoungreaders.com

Cataloging-in-Publication Data is available on
the Library of Congress website.
ISBN: 978-1-4965-0519-4 (reinforced library bound)
ISBN: 978-1-4965-0524-8 (paperback)
ISBN: 978-1-4965-2328-0 (eBook)

Summary: Despite his name, ten-year-old Jim Nasium
is a phys ed klutz. But he's not stopping until he finds the right
sport for him in this whacky chapter book adventure! Now he's
ready to lace up some skates! Will Jim Nasium be a hockey hazard
or a rink rock star?

Printed in the United States of America in North Mankato, Minnesota.
022016   009565R

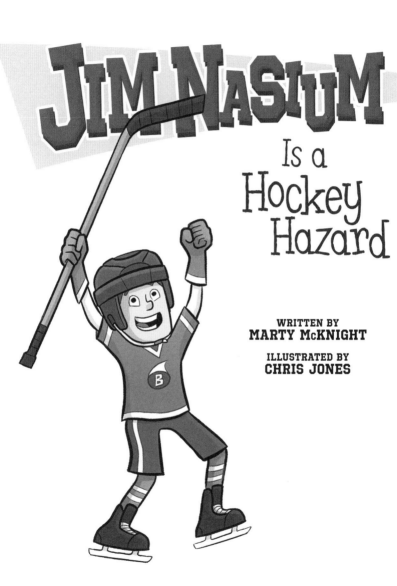

JIM NASIUM

Is a Hockey Hazard

WRITTEN BY
MARTY McKNIGHT

ILLUSTRATED BY
CHRIS JONES

CONTENTS

CHAPTER ONE

COLD FEET

I stood on the ice at the Bennett Elementary Ice Rink with two dozen classmates. My gym teacher Coach Pittman had handed out flyers the day before. They read: "Join the Buffalo hockey team. More information tomorrow at 2:30 p.m. Don't be late!"

The scoreboard clock ticked to 2:29.

The waiting was driving me CRAZY!

My teeth chattered, my hands shook, and my legs quivered. I couldn't tell if I was nervous to get started or just really, really chilly.

Do I have cold feet or are my feet just cold? I wondered.

Exactly one minute later, Coach Pittman skated onto the ice. He circled the arena like a speed skater and then came to a quick stop in front of us.

SHOOOOSH! The blades of his skates dug into the ice, spraying our shoes with slush.

Everyone cheered. My classmates couldn't wait to strap on their own skates. I wish I could've said the same. My skating skills weren't exactly — well, they weren't SKILLS at all, really.

"Calm down, gentlemen," said the coach. "We have a few things to discuss before we hit the ice."

"I'll be hitting the ice, all right," I told my best friend, Milo. "Probably with my face. Or my butt."

"Is there a difference?" our archenemy Bobby Studwell chimed in.

"HAHAHA! Good one, Bobby," said his super-annoying sidekick, Tommy Strong.

"Quiet down, you four!" shouted Coach Pittman. He held his fingertips to his mouth and made a turning motion. "Zip up your mouths and throw away the keys."

"The hocKEYS, right, Coach?" said Milo, grinning.

The boys all laughed.

BREEEEP! Coach blew his whistle.

"All right, all right. That's enough," he said. "I see you all brought your permission slips. Bring them up, and I'll check off your names."

One by one, the boys shuffled across the ice toward the coach.

I didn't move.

I looked down at my permission slip. My hand was shaking so hard, I could barely read my dad's signature.

I definitely have cold feet, I thought.

Seconds later, Milo spoke up. "Ahem!" he grunted, jabbing his elbow into my ribs. "What are you waiting for, Jim?" Then he shoved me forward.

I slid gracefully across the ice in my tennis shoes, spinning like an Olympic figure skater before coming to a perfect stop in front of Coach Pittman.

"Nice footwork, Jim Nasium," said Coach, checking my name off the list. "See you at practice tomorrow."

***

You heard him right. The name's Jim Nasium — don't wear it out!

With a name like mine I should be a sports sensation. You know, a real gym class hero!

The problem is . . . I lack some serious game.

You've heard that old saying "born with two left feet." Well, I was born with two left feet AND two left arms! That's a real problem in hockey — or any sport, for that matter.

And I'd know. At this point, I've tried just about every sport on the entire planet.

The result?

Well, let's just say I've warmed some very nice benches in my day.

But this year is going to be different.

This year, I won't be a hockey hazard. I'll be a rink rock star!

CHAPTER TWO

POND SCUM

Later that afternoon, I met Milo and a few friends at the park. Ever since the temperatures dropped, we'd been facing off against each other in boot hockey on the local pond.

Boot hockey is exactly what it sounds like. It's hockey but with BOOTS instead of SKATES. And I used my boots to kick some serious butt!

Too bad boot hockey isn't an actual sport, because I'd be an all-star.

So why was I worried about joining the school's hockey team?

Well, it's not my FOOTwork I'm worried about. It's my SKATEwork! Put me in a pair of skates, and I'm like a fish out of water — I mean, ice.

"Pass me the puck, Jim!" I suddenly heard Milo shout. I looked up and spotted Milo shuffling across the pond toward a goal made of milk crates.

We had twenty-eight seconds left in a two-on-two matchup. We'd played every night that week, and the series was tied two games apiece.

It was Friday, and this was the deciding game. Whoever won would take home the ultimate prize: a triple-chocolate doughnut with multi-colored sprinkles from Milo's lunch box.

The doughnut seemed like a much better prize on Monday, but victory would still taste pretty sweet (even if the doughnut probably wouldn't).

"Heads up, Milo!" I shouted.

I jammed my hockey stick behind the puck and flicked my wrists. The puck skittered across the ice, connecting with Milo's stick on the other side of the pond.

"Nice pass!" Milo shouted back.

Milo shuffled toward the goal, controlling the tiny puck with his stick. Our opponents, the Ted-and-Ned twins, slid after him in their boots.

But Milo was too quick. As he approached the goal, Milo raised his stick for his famous slapshot.

THWACK!! He slapped the puck toward the goal. The puck spun end over end and then **BONK!** It bounced off one of the milk crates and back toward Ted and Ned.

"Uh-oh!" Milo exclaimed.

"Got it!" I said, zipping between everyone and rebounding the puck right in front of the goal.

I poked my hockey stick forward and gently nudged the puck. It slid right between the milk crates for the game-winning shot! The timer on Milo's cell phone sounded.

Milo tore off his stocking cap and threw it onto the ice. "Way to go, Jim!" he shouted. "That's a hat trick!"

"Huh?" I asked, puzzled.

"A hat trick," Milo repeated. "That's what they call it when a player scores three goals in one game. It's a hockey tradition to throw your hat on the ice when it happens."

I threw my hat on the ice.

"Feels great, doesn't it?" Milo asked.

"Feels cold," I replied, picking up my stocking cap and quickly tugging it back on.

"Good game, guys," said the Ted-and-Ned twins in unison.

Ted reached down, picked up Milo's lunch box off of the ice, and opened it. "To the winners . . ." he began.

"Go the spoils," Ned finished.

"You got that right," I said, peeking into the lunch box.

At the bottom sat a graying, week-old doughnut — at least I think it was a doughnut! This looked more like a mushy mush of a brain, with fuzzy caterpillar-like sprinkles on top.

"Yuck!" I exclaimed. "It's all yours, buddy." I gave Milo a pat on the back.

Milo licked his lips and then grabbed the spoiled treat. "Mmm." He drooled. "Doughnut mind if I do."

"Not so fast," said Bobby Studwell, skating up and snatching the doughnut from Milo's hand.

"Hey!" shouted the Ted-and-Ned twins together.

"Well, if it isn't the Pond Scum," Milo joked as Tommy Strong joined us on the ice, too.

"And to think I was about to share this tasty treat with you all," said Bobby, about to bite the doughnut.

"Bobby, don't eat that," I warned.

"Don't worry, Nasium," Bobby replied. "I'll save you the center." He placed a finger through the doughnut hole and laughed.

"HAHAHA! Good one, Bobby," Tommy exclaimed.

"But that doughnut is —" I started.

"What, Nasium? WHAT?" Bobby interrupted.

I thought for a moment and smiled. "Never mind. It's all yours, Bobby."

"Finally something we agree on," said Bobby, shoving the whole doughnut into his big mouth.

CHAPTER THREE

SOCKEY

"JIMMMM!!!" my dad shouted up from the laundry room.

We had just finished dinner, and I was sweeping the kitchen floor. I could hear my dad stomping up the basement steps.

"Jim, what is this?" he asked, appearing at the top of the stairs.

He was holding a basket full of dirty laundry. My jeans from that day were crumpled on top.

"What's what?" I asked.

Dad set down the laundry basket and held up my jeans. "This vomit-colored stuff on your brand-new pants," he replied.

"Oh," I said. "That's vomit."

"Yuck!" Dad shouted, throwing the pants back into the basket. "How about a heads-up next time, Jim?"

He picked up the laundry basket, and a balled-up pair of socks fell to the ground. They skittered across the wood floor toward me.

"Got it, Dad!" I exclaimed.

Using the kitchen broom, I batted the sock ball like a hockey puck. I pushed the socks around the kitchen floor, down the hallway, and then back toward Dad.

"MEOOOOOOW!"

My cat Vinnie chased alongside. He swiped at the puck with his razor-sharp claws. I zigged and zagged, keeping just out of his reach.

"Wow!" my dad exclaimed. "You've really gotten good, Jim! The hockey team will be lucky to have you."

"Thanks, Dad. But —" I stopped.

"But what, Jim?" asked Dad.

"Well, it's not my puckhandling that I'm worried about," I said, weaving the sock-puck in and out of the dining-room furniture. "It's my skating skills."

"What about them?" Dad asked.

"I don't have any!" I exclaimed.

"Maybe it's not you," my dad suggested. "Maybe your equipment is holding you back. Let's head over to the sporting goods store tomorrow before practice. A new pair of skates might be just what the doctor ordered."

"Really? Thanks, Dad!" I shouted. "I promise you won't be disappointed."

I glanced down at the sock-puck on the kitchen floor. Then I pulled the broom back behind my head and swung it forward.

WHACK! I unleashed a monster slapshot. The sock-puck rocketed across the kitchen toward my dad.

THWAP! The makeshift puck struck him right on the melon. It bounced off his forehead and fell into the laundry basket in his hands.

Dad frowned. "Like I said, son, a little heads-up would be nice." Then he wiped his forehead with the back of his hand and gave it a sniff. "Wait — what's on these socks?!"

CHAPTER FOUR

SHOP TILL THE PUCK DROPS

The next morning, Dad, Milo, and I piled into the minivan and headed to the sporting goods store. I still wasn't sure that a new pair of skates would make me a good skater, but I'd give anything a shot!

As we walked through the aisles, we passed a section of used equipment.

"Dad, look at this baseball mitt!" I exclaimed. "It's super expensive at the mall, but it's only ten dollars here!"

I shoved my hand into the used mitt and pounded my fist into the webbing a couple times. It felt great.

"And it fits like a glove, Jim." Milo laughed. "Get it?"

My dad looked puzzled. Then, after a moment he exclaimed, "Oh, HA! I get it, Milo! HAHA!" He turned to me. "Throw the glove in the basket. It's worth the money just for the joke!"

"You sure that's okay, Dad?" I asked. "We're here for hockey equipment, remember?"

"Of course! You'll need it for baseball next spring," Dad replied. "Let's just hope your hands don't grow too much. Otherwise, that glove won't fit like a glove anymore. Ain't that right, Milo?" He jabbed Milo with his elbow and chuckled.

Milo and I both groaned.

I threw the glove into our shopping basket. Then we headed to the hockey aisle. Sticks, pads, helmets, and skates were stacked floor to ceiling.

"Try these on for size, Jim," said Dad, holding up a pair of shiny black-and-silver skates.

"Wow! These are great!" I said.

I ran my fingers over the white laces and studied the razor-sharp blades. Then I wrestled the skates onto my feet. My feet sunk into the cushy, warm padding inside.

At least part of my cold-feet problem is solved, I thought.

I stood, balancing on the blades, and asked Dad, "What do you think?"

"Hey, Jim!" came a voice from behind.

I spun, tripped, and fell to the floor with a *THUD!*

When I looked up, I spotted a familiar face standing over me. "Bobby Studwell," I grumbled.

"Hey, Nasium," said Bobby, "the figure skates are over there." He pointed to the other side of the store.

"Well then I guess you made a wrong turn," Milo chimed in, smiling.

"Always the wise guy, Cabrera," Bobby sneered.

"Oh my, I'm so sorry! I'm so sorry!" shouted a woman as she ran up to us. "Did my little Bobby-Poo do this?"

"Bobby-Poo?" said Milo, puzzled.

We both snorted with laughter.

"My little Bobby-Poo isn't himself today," she explained. "His tummy-wummy is feeling queasy-weezy."

The lady rustled Bobby's blond hair and then kissed his cheek.

"MOMMM!!" Bobby cried. "Stop!"

"Anyway," continued Mrs. Studwell, "I thought some new skates would make him feel better."

"We had the same idea," my dad chimed in. "I'm Jim's father." He shook Mrs. Studwell's hand and then turned to Bobby. "And you are?"

"Bobby," he groaned.

"Nice to meet you, Bobby. Jim's mentioned you before," said my dad. "You two must be good friends."

"I'm going to be sick," said Bobby.

"Manners!" shouted Bobby's mother.

I stared at Bobby. He looked dizzy and his face was turning green.

"No I think he's actually going to be sick," I told everyone.

Bobby's eyes went wide. He frantically searched for a toilet, a bucket, a trash can — or, a shopping basket!

"Dad! Heads up!" I shouted.

BLAAAAHHHHHHH!

CHAPTER FIVE

DOWN AND OUT?

Before heading home to start another load of puke-covered laundry, Dad dropped Milo and me off at the school's ice arena. Today was the first official day of hockey practice!

Everyone piled into the locker room, carrying new skates, pads, masks, sticks, and pucks.

I shoved my equipment into a locker next to Milo. Then we both took a seat on the bench and waited for Coach.

Moments later, Bobby Studwell stepped into the room. He had a brand-new pair of XZR 3000 hockey skates slung over his shoulder.

Apparently, even the best skates money could buy hadn't cheered him up. Bobby's face was still the color of, well, pond scum.

"How are you feeling . . . Bobby-Poo?" Milo asked, snickering.

Bobby stepped toward Milo. "I'll be feeling a lot better when we face off on the ice," he growled.

"If you can keep up," Milo added. "Jim here's a boot hockey MVP!"

"Well, this isn't BOOT hockey, Cabrera," Bobby said.

He's right, I thought, still nervous about lacing up my skates.

"Maybe not," said Milo, "but both sports use a stick and a puck."

Milo tossed me a hockey stick and then threw a puck into the air.

Without thinking, I quickly stuck out the stick, batting the puck back into the air before it hit the ground. I did this over and over again, until all of my teammates had gathered around to watch me.

"Wow!" said one kid.

"He's really good!" I heard another teammate say.

For the first time I could remember, I really did feel like an MVP.

Then . . . *YOINK!*

Coach Pittman snatched the puck out of midair. "That's enough horseplay, gentlemen," he said, slipping the puck into his pocket.

"Um, Coach?" Milo asked, raising his hand. "Don't you mean BUFFALOplay? We are the Bennett City Buffaloes, after all!"

The team all laughed.

(I'd heard the joke a thousand times, but it still cracked me up, too.)

The team stomped their feet, clapped their hands, and let out the Bennett City battle cry.

BUUUURRRRRRRRRRRP!

The battle cry was supposed to sound like a buffalo grunt. But it always sounded more like a giant belch to me.

BREEEEEP! Coach blew his whistle and everyone went silent.

"We don't have time for *any* kind of play," Coach explained. "Our first game against the Dodge City Dinos is in a week. They have the winningest coach in state hockey history."

Coach held up a newspaper article about the Dinos' coach. The headline read: RECORD BREAKER! Next to the article was a picture of an old, bald man with inch-thick glasses and a walking cane.

"Whoa!" Milo exclaimed. "No wonder he has the most wins in state hockey history. That Dino coach is prehistoric!"

"HAHAHAHA!" the team laughed.

BREEEEEEEP! Coach blew his whistle again

"A little respect, gentlemen," said Coach. "Old equals experience, something most of you lack."

Coach Pittman turned and headed out of the locker room. "But we're going to change that," he said, exiting the door. "Strap on your skates and meet me on the ice in five minutes."

I opened my locker and pulled out my shiny black-and-silver skates.

What's the worst that could happen? I thought.

Unfortunately, I was about to find out. Because a moment later, I was lined up on one side of the hockey rink with my teammates.

"On my whistle," Coach said, "I want you to race down and touch the boards on the other side of the rink."

Ready, set, **BREEEEEEEEEEEEEEP!**

I pushed off, skated hard, and quickly took the lead. *Hey,* I thought, *I think I have the hang of this.*

But as I neared the other side, I realized one thing . . .

I didn't know how to stop!

CRAAAASH! I smashed into the boards like a two-ton elephant hitting a two-ton truck.

"Man down," Bobby joked, sliding to a perfect stop beside me.

Coach Pittman skated up too. "You okay, Nasium?" he asked.

"Define 'okay,'" I replied.

"Why don't you hit the showers for today," he suggested.

"But I didn't even break a sweat, Coach," I told him.

"Well, then skip the shower," he said, "but maybe you should sit this one out."

I'm down, all right, I thought. *Down AND out.*

CHAPTER SIX

TIME TO CHANGE

I shuffled back into the locker room, hanging my head. Maybe Bobby was right. Maybe my boot hockey skills weren't enough to make me a rink rock star. After all, I was a boot hockey champion. But after only one day of ice hockey, well, I'd just been given the boot.

I opened my locker and slumped down on the bench. Then I took off my Buffaloes jersey and pads.

Maybe it's not just time to change clothes, I thought. *Maybe it's time for a change.*

Like I said, I'd tried just about every sport on the planet, and where had all that hard work gotten me? Right back where I started: the bench.

Frustrated, I tore off my skates and tossed them into the back of the locker.

WHAM!

A ball of socks fell down from the top shelf of the locker and bounced onto the floor.

"If only I was as good at real sports as I was at fake sports," I told myself. "Like Sockey!" (Yep! I'd given my fake sport a name.)

I grabbed my hockey stick and started dribbling the sock-puck around the locker room. I zigged and zagged through the showers, over benches, and under open locker doors, all while controlling the sock-puck. I felt like an NHL all-star!

"You know what?" I asked myself. "I'm not giving up. Dad's right. This team would be lucky to have me."

I glared at the sock-puck and pulled back my stick.

"By the end of the week," I proclaimed, "I'll earn some respect."

THWACK!

I slapped the puck toward the locker room door. Just then, Coach Pittman stepped inside, and the sock-puck struck him right between the eyes.

"Gulp!"

Bobby wasn't the only one feeling sick.

CHAPTER SEVEN

IT FIGURES

So apparently the coach never wanted me off the team. He really did just want me to rest up. And, thankfully, he was also pretty cool about the whole getting-hit-in-the-face-with-a-dirty-sock thing.

All was good. Oh, except for the fact that I still couldn't skate.

Coach suggested I stay after practice for a few nights and "get a feel for the ice," as he put it.

I didn't say it to the coach, but I already knew how the ice felt . . .

HARD.

I decided he was right. So that afternoon, after the team had packed up and headed home, Milo and I headed back out to the rink.

Unfortunately, the ice was already being used by a half dozen seven-year-old girls and boys.

"Hey, isn't that your sister?" I asked Milo, pointing at a little girl with a ponytail.

"Oh yeah," he said, squinting through his thick glasses. "I forgot that she had practice today."

"Practice?" I asked, puzzled.

"Meg is on the Tiny Twirlers," Milo replied.

"Huh?"

"The Tiny Twirlers is a beginners figure skating team," he explained.

"That's just great," I said. "Let's get out of here, Milo. The last thing I need is to watch a bunch of other kids who can't skate."

"I wouldn't be so sure about that," Milo told me.

He pointed at his sister, who was skating toward us at full speed.

As Meg reached center ice, she bent her legs and dug her skate blades into the ice. Then she leaped into the air, spinning once, twice, maybe THREE times before landing perfectly.

"WOW!" Milo and I exclaimed.

"Was that a, uh, triple axel?" I asked Milo. It was the only skating trick I'd learned while watching the Winter Olympics.

"Looks more like a double cheeseburger to me," said Milo.

"Cheeseburger?" I asked, puzzled.

"Yeah," he said, pointing toward the concession stand on the other side of the arena. "Care to join me?"

"In a minute," I replied. "I think I forgot something in the locker room."

I hadn't really forgotten anything. As Milo walked away, I tried to get Meg's attention on the ice.

"Psst," I whispered, hoping no one else would notice me. "Psst! Meg!"

Finally she heard me. "JIM!" Meg shouted from the other side of the rink. Everyone in the arena turned in my direction — except for Milo, of course. He was already on his third double cheeseburger.

Meg gracefully skated over. "What's up, Jim?" she asked. "Shouldn't you be scarfing down burgers with my brother? He's already on number four."

I looked over, and Milo had already downed another one.

"I wish I could," I began, "but I need your help."

"Me?" Meg asked, curious. "What do you need my help for?"

I looked from side to side to make sure nobody was listening. "I need you to teach me how to skate."

"HA!" Meg laughed. "But you're on the hockey team. Why would you need me to teach you how to skate?"

"Because I'm on the hockey team," I explained.

"Oh," said Meg, finally realizing what I was telling her.

"So can you help?" I asked.

"We have our first figure-skating competition in a week, and I'm not sure I'll have time," she explained. "Unless . . ."

"Unless what?" I asked.

"We need some more older skaters on the Tiny Twirlers," said Meg. "If you join the team, I can practice and teach you at the same time!"

I wasn't sure I had a choice.

CHAPTER EIGHT

LEAPS AND BOUNDS

During the next week, I stuck with hockey. Then right after practice, I would join the Tiny Twirlers, where I learned to stick my landings.

"Remember, Jim, keep your eyes straight ahead," Meg instructed on the day before the game. "Whatever you do, don't look down at your skates."

I looked down at my skates.

My legs wobbled, and my skates started sliding in two different directions. "Whoa!" I exclaimed, extending my arms for balance.

"What did I just say?" growled Meg, crossing her arms in frustration.

Meg was a lot like Coach Pittman. They were both tough. But, if you were willing to listen, their instructions actually helped.

When I first started training with the Tiny Twirlers, I could barely stand up (or stop!). Within a week, my skating skills were growing by leaps and bounds — no joke!

"Okay, Jim," said Meg, "now show me what you've got."

Just as Meg had done a few days earlier, I skated across the rink at full speed. When I reached center ice, I bent my knees, dug in my blades, and leaped into the air.

WHOOSH! WHOOSH! WHOOSH!

I completed three rotations in midair (well, maybe it was only one, but it felt like three!). My skates finally touched the ground again, and —

WHAM-O! I smashed into the ice like a dizzy penguin.

"Uhn," I groaned, getting up.

Meg quickly skated over and patted me on the back. "Nice work, Jim!"

"Huh? Didn't you see me fall?" I said, holding my ribs and trying to catch my breath. "That was awful!"

"Yes, but you nearly did it," said Meg. "Just a few adjustments, and you'll be landing that jump every time. What you're feeling right now is the feeling of hard work and success."

I hugged my ribs tighter and thought, *If this is success, I'd hate to know what failure feels like.*

CHAPTER NINE

FACING OFF

The next day, I feared I might find out exactly that. Failure still felt like a real possibility. Although I'd improved, I had still only been practicing for a week with the Tiny Twirlers.

Is that enough to turn a hockey hazard into a rink rock star? I wondered. Only time would tell.

Luckily, I had plenty of that on my hands. Throughout the first and second period, Coach Pittman assigned me to my most valuable position: sitting on my butt.

I have to admit I could barely concentrate on the game. As the third period ticked away, I kept looking down at my skates and thinking about all the advice Meg had given me.

Her voice shouted in my brain: "Whatever you do, don't look down at your skates!"

Oops! I shook my head and looked up. When I did, I saw Bobby Studwell score and heard the buzzer sound.

BREEEEEEEEEP!

Then I heard Coach shout, "Jim Nasium, you're in!"

"Isn't the game over?" I asked.

"HAHA!" Bobby laughed. "It might as well be if you're coming into the game, Nasium," he growled.

I ignored Bobby and looked up at the clock on the scoreboard. Only twenty-eight seconds remained in the third period.

I remembered our boot hockey tournament from the week before.

That's just enough time to become this game's MVP, I thought.

Whether MVP would stand for Most Valuable Player or Most VALUELESS Player would be left up to me.

CHAPTER TEN

EMPTY NETTER

Before I could think better, I slowly skated out to center ice. Bobby lined up for the face-off. I line up to the right of him, as right winger. Milo lined up to the left of him, as left winger.

"Hey, Jim!" Bobby called. "How is a bad hockey player like the *Titanic*?"

I shrugged my shoulders.

"They are terrible as soon as they hit the ice!" He laughed.

"HAHAHA! Very funny," Milo said from the other side of the ice. "But you really shouldn't tell jokes during a hockey game, Bobby."

"Yeah, and why's that, Cabrera?" asked Bobby.

"Because the ice might crack up!" Milo howled.

Everyone laughed — even the Dinos players!

BREEEEEEEEP!

The referee blew his whistle and held a puck in the air.

The arena went silent until —

PLINK! — the puck hit the ice and the clock started.

Twenty-seven . . . Twenty-six . . .

CRASH! KLaNK! Bobby batted sticks with the Dinos' center until the puck finally came lose. It skittered over to the left side of the rink, and Milo took control.

Twenty . . . Nineteen . . .

Phew, I thought.

I was somewhat relieved. With less than twenty seconds remaining, I just had to avoid the puck. I'd have another whole week to practice with the Tiny Twirlers.

Just then, I heard Milo call out, "Heads up, Jim!"

He jammed his hockey stick behind the puck and flicked his wrists. The puck floated across the ice toward me.

TWACK! The puck hit the blade of my stick and stuck there like glue.

I looked up at the scoreboard clock. "Uh-oh," I said.

Ten . . . Nine . . .

"Show me what you've got, Jim!" I heard a tiny voice from the stands.

It was Meg. She was sitting in the bleachers behind the goal, wearing a sparkling uniform and smiling.

Five . . . Four . . .

I pushed off the ice with my skates, controlling the puck in front of me. I didn't look down. I imagined gliding across the pond on a worn pair of boots. I imagined pushing a sock-puck across my kitchen floor.

Only one Dino defensive player stood between me and the goal. As I skated closer, the player crouched low, ready to check me into the boards.

I crouched low too. But right before we collided, I extended my legs like a spring. I leaped into the air, spinning once, twice (maybe THREE times!), right over the top of the Dino player.

Three . . . Two . . .

I stuck the landing perfectly, coming down right behind the puck. I immediately controlled the puck again, and then looked up at the goal ahead.

Where's the goalie? I wondered, spotting an open net in front of me.

One . . .

I didn't wait for an answer. I pulled my stick back behind my head and unleashed a superpowered slapshot.

KA-POW! The puck rocketed into the net and the final buzzer sounded.

BREEEEEEEEEEEP!

"You did it!" Milo exclaimed, skating up and giving me a high-five.

My other teammates crowded around as well. They cheered, slapping me on the helmet and shoulder pads.

"Nice work, Nasium," said Bobby. "We obviously couldn't have won this game without you." He pointed up at the scoreboard.

The final score read:

Dinos 0

Buffaloes 7

So I guess I wasn't a rink rock star, after all. But I wasn't a hockey hazard either, and that felt pretty good

Just then, an old, bald man with inch-thick glasses and a walking cane shuffled onto the ice. It was the coach of the Dodge City Dinos.

(Milo had been right. He did look a bit prehistoric.)

"In all my years, I haven't seen anything like that," he said, shaking my hand. "Well, maybe during the 1909 championship game. But back then we didn't have sticks or pucks or ice. We used a rolled-up ball of socks! Can you believe that, sonny?"

I laughed.

"Anyway, congratulations," he said. "You have my respect."

"To celebrate," Coach Pittman chimed in, "I'm taking you all out for doughnuts!"

Everyone cheered — except Bobby, who gagged a little.

"As much as I love doughnuts, Coach," I told him, "there's something I have to do."

Just then, I removed my hockey uniform to reveal a shiny, sequined figure-skating uniform beneath. Then Meg and the other Tiny Twirlers joined me on the ice.

I smiled and said, "My team is counting on me!"

AUTHOR

Marty McKnight is a freelance writer from St. Paul, Minnesota. He has written many chapter books for young readers.

ILLUSTRATOR

Chris Jones is a children's illustrator based in Canada. He has worked as both a graphic designer and an illustrator. His illustrations have appeared in several magazines and educational publications, and he also has numerous graphic novels and children's books to his credit. Chris is inspired by good music, books, long walks, and generous amounts of coffee.

HOCKEY JOKES!

Q: Why was the zombie thrown out of the hockey game?

A: He had a face off on the ice.

Q: Why are magicians great hockey players?

A: They have the best hat tricks!

Q: What kind of fish plays hockey?

A: A skate.

Q: How is a bad hockey player like the *Titanic*?

A: They were terrible as soon as they hit the ice!

Q: What's the difference between a judge and a hockey rink?

A: One is a bringer of justice, and the other is just ice.

Q: Why couldn't the math teacher wear hockey skates?

A: He only had square feet!

Q: Where's the best place to buy a hockey uniform?

A: New Jersey!

Q: What's the first thing frogs do when they play hockey?

A: They get on their pads!